For Lily Elizabeth Waterfield x—M. R.

For Heather and Tony x—N. E.

First edition for the United States, and its
territories and dependencies, published
in 2015 by B.E.S. Publishing Co.

First published in Great Britain in 2014 by Puffin Books
Penguin Books Ltd
80 Strand
London WC2R 0RL
Great Britain

All inquiries should be addressed to:
B.E.S. Publishing Co.
250 Wireless Boulevard
Hauppauge, NY 11788
www.bes-publishing.com

ISBN: 978-1-4380-0663-5

Library of Congress Control Number:
2014945558

Date of Manufacture: December 2019
Manufactured by: RR Donnelley Asia Printing
Solutions Limited

Product conforms to all applicable ASTM F-963
and all applicable CPSC and CPSIA 2008 standards.
No lead or phthalate hazard.

Printed in China
9 8

Goodnight Princess

PUBLISHING

Michelle Robinson

Illustrated by **Nick East**

The stars are out,
the moon is bright.
It's time to dream.
Let's say goodnight.

Goodnight necklace.

Goodnight crown.

Goodnight slippers.

Goodnight gown.

Goodnight throne,
and goodnight dress.
Time for bed.

Goodnight princess.

Goodnight palace.
Goodnight king.

Goodnight pony.

Goodnight
ring

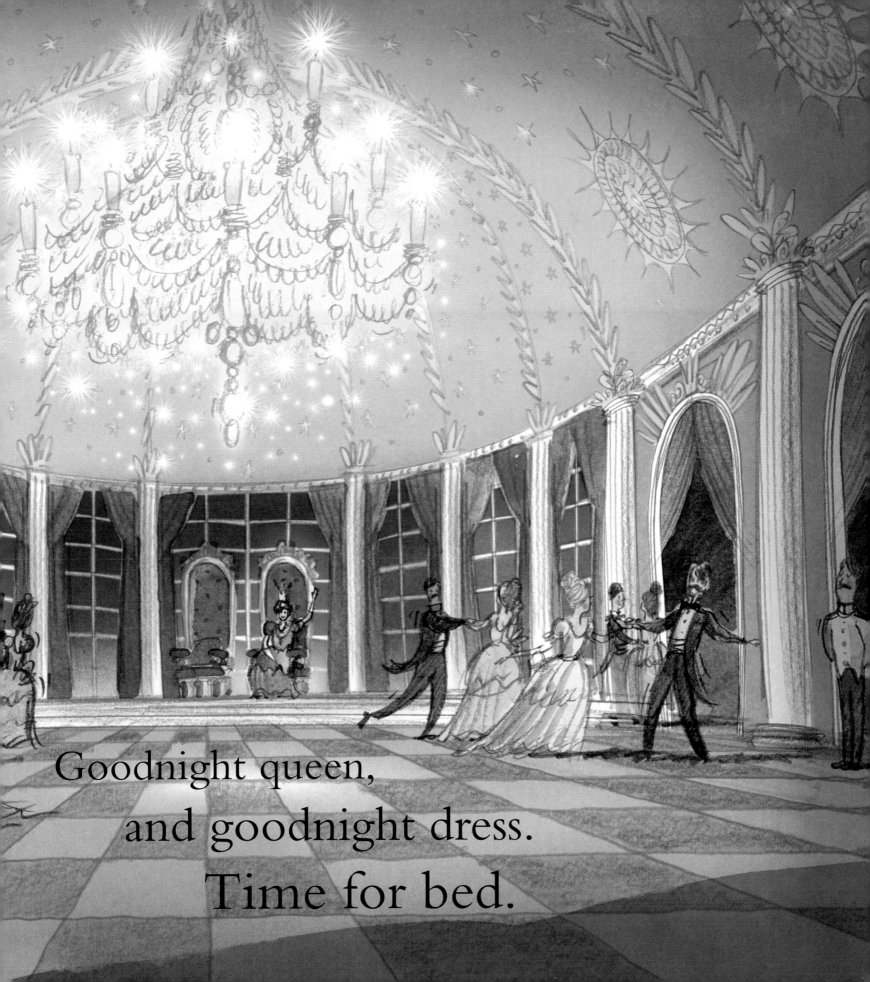

Goodnight queen,
and goodnight dress.
Time for bed.

Goodnight princess.

Goodnight fairies.
Goodnight flowers.

Goodnight balls
and belles in towers.

Necklace, dresses, gems, and rings.

Posies, ponies, queens, and kings.

Magic slippers,
balls
and
gowns.

Moon
and
stars
and sparkly crowns.

Goodnight all, and goodnight dress.

Time for bed.

Goodnight princess.